Felix Takes the Blame

by Maeve Friel

Cardiff Libraries
www.cardiff.gov.uk/libraries

Llyfrgelloedd Caerdydd
www.caerdydd.gov.uk/llyfrgelloedd

Illustrated by Beccy Blake

W

A   D0414154

First published in 2010 by
Franklin Watts
338 Euston Road
London
NW1 3BH

Franklin Watts Australia
Level 17/207 Kent Street
Sydney
NSW 2000

Text © Maeve Friel 2010
Illustration © Beccy Blake 2010

The rights of Maeve Friel to be identified as the author
and Beccy Blake as the illustrator of this Work have been
asserted in accordance with the Copyright, Designs and
Patents Act, 1988.

All rights reserved. No part of this publication may be
reproduced, stored in a retrieval system, or transmitted
in any form or by any means, electronic, mechanical,
photocopy, recording or otherwise, without the prior
written permission of the copyright owner.

A CIP catalogue record for this book is available
from the British Library.

ISBN 978 0 7496 9456 2 (hbk)
ISBN 978 0 7496 9466 1 (pbk)

Series Editor: Jackie Hamley
Series Advisor: Catherine Glavina
Series Designer: Peter Scoulding

Printed in China

Franklin Watts is a divison of
Hachette Children's Books,
an Hachette UK company.
www.hachette.co.uk

For Ciara Maeve Kennedy
with love from Granny Maeve

Felix got blamed
for everything.

CRASH!

3

"FELIX! Where's Felix? Did you do this?" shouted Mum.

"Me? No. No. I didn't do it!"
Felix protested.

Oh no! Not again!

"Look at these sheets!" said Dad. "Where's that cat?"

"But it wasn't me. I didn't do it!" miaowed Felix.

"This is too much. FELIX!
I'm very cross with you,"
Mum yelled.

12

"But I wasn't even here!"
Felix fumed.

"Honestly! Felix, I've told you before. You must not dig up my tomato plants," grumbled Dad.

17

"But it wasn't me! I never dig up the plants! It was Buster!"

Felix was very angry.

"Why do I always get the blame?" he miaowed crossly.

"What a mess!" said
Mum. "It can't be — poo.
Oh really, Felix. You're
disgraceful."

Felix stopped washing his face. "I didn't do it," he miaowed. "It wasn't me. Not me. Never."

Suki the kitten was chasing a butterfly.

Felix pointed a paw.
"It was ..."

Everyone looked at Felix.
"Who was it?" they said.

Felix looked at Suki.

"It was me," he miaowed.

And he turned a little red.

29

Puzzle 1

Put these pictures in the correct order.
Now tell the story in your own words.
How short can you make the story?

Puzzle 2

upset   confused

delighted

angry   tired

cross

Choose the words which best describe each character. Can you think of any more? Pretend to be one of the characters!

Answers

Puzzle 1

The correct order is:

1c, 2f, 3a, 4e, 5d, 6b

Puzzle 2

Felix The correct words are confused, upset.
The incorrect word is delighted.

Mum The correct words are angry, cross.
The incorrect word is tired.

Look out for more Leapfrog stories:

For details of all our titles go to: www.franklinwatts.co.uk

*hardback